MW01705009

The Lighthouse in Grove Park School

Mary K Slimmer

Mary K Slimmer

Copyright © 2012 Author Name

All rights reserved.

ISBN:0615705367
ISBN-13:978-0615705361

DEDICATION

FOR MY FAMILY

Notes

This book is a work of fiction. Names, characters, businesses, organizations, events, places and incidents either are a product of the author's imagination or are used fictitiously. Any resemblance to actual persons, living or dead, events, or locales is entirely coincidental.

Cover created by Misty Mosher Slimmer

ACKNOWLEDGMENTS

This book has been inspired by many who have given me encouragement, constructive criticism, wonderful ideas, and hope that I really could take on this endeavor. My heartfelt thanks to:

my grandchildren: Brady Slimmer, Presley Slimmer, Andrew Bush and Dominic Reynolds who listened intently to the story and shared their thoughts and ideas with me.

my children: Kevin Slimmer and his fiancée Kristen Segal, Kim and Jeff Reynolds, and Kris and Misty Slimmer who kept asking about the progress of this book and showed their sincere interest in its completion.

my friends who bragged about me to others and made me feel special.

my writing group: Jim Farfaglia, and June and Phil McArthur who took the time to read the rough draft and offered such wonderful criticism along the way. They believed that I was a writer.

my husband, Milt Slimmer, to whom I owe my sincere thanks because he patiently listened at the dining room table, in the car, on the porch, or wherever, to help my story sound believable. He always was ready to listen.

1 CHAPTER

I could feel the sweat on my neck. My chest vibrated from the pounding. I was sure everyone in the police station could hear it. My parents were on their way and I was hoping they would arrive before Mrs. Lutnam confronted us. I knew I was in big trouble but I was hoping my parents would understand. Mrs. Lutnam, our principal, was standing in the outer office of the police station waiting for our parents to arrive. I had never seen her look so upset.

I heard the anxiety in my father's shaky voice talking to Mrs. Lutnam. I covered my ears and closed my eyes. But when I heard my mom gently calling my name, I looked up to find her. I ran into her arms and flooded her with tears. We were looking into each others' eyes. And finally, the unbroken silence became awkward. Mom pointed me in the direction of a small private room where the police station office stored supplies and kept the copier. We both sat down. As I was searching for the words, I reflected on how this all started.

My name is Emily Binda. I have attended Grove Park Elementary School since kindergarten. This is where I met Laura and Christina. We became friends right away. It was a forced friendship at first because we were assigned to the same work table every day. Since Kindergarten we three have been assigned to the same class and since then, we have formed a solid, everlasting friendship. I wonder if our parents had something to do with that.

I was lucky if I owned three pair of jeans. My mom shopped at a used clothing store for me. I was always afraid someone in my school would recognize something that I was wearing. My mom didn't work outside the house so she was always at home baking cakes, playing the Wii when she had time, and taking care of everything. I liked it that way. It was really nice to go home every day knowing she was there.

We were the best of friends all through elementary school. The three of us were very different, but we weren't afraid to be ourselves around each other. Laura was the pretty one with long blonde hair that glistened when the sun filtered through her hair as she passed the windows in the corridor. Most of the time, she bounced from place to place with a smile that recharged anyone who saw her. But I knew the truth behind her winning smiles. She never told me right out but I knew why she wore long sleeves on warm days. And I could guess why she stared out the window with an empty gaze during Math class.

Christina was the one who loved horses. She lived in the country and shared tales of her family's outings; riding horses together and picnicking near the huge lake that surrounded our community. Laura and I loved hearing her stories. When she was in school she would often go to an empty table in the cafeteria for lunch. She liked to be alone but we didn't let her sit there alone for long. We knew she loved our company and I always saved apple slices from my lunch for her. We were lucky not to get caught switching tables by the grumpy lunch lady.

The boys in our classrooms have always been so whiny. We really didn't even notice them until the beginning of last year when we were all in fifth grade. My grades were always good until fifth grade. Then it really seemed hard to get my homework done every night. I couldn't stop thinking about Mark and Joe. They were so cool. They wore different clothes to school every day.

So now we are in sixth grade. My parents have

challenged me to get better grades this year by promising me a trip to Disneyland if I got on the honor roll at least three times this year. So far, I have accomplished this feat for the first two grading periods. It hasn't been easy. Christina has really helped me. She is brilliant and has a way of helping me understand stuff. She would make a great teacher some day. It has really been hard to focus on schoolwork too. After all, Mark, Alan and Joe are in our class this year.

Laura came to class late one day this week. I saw her going into the principal's office on our way to class as the first bell of the day was clamoring. I tried to catch up to her, but I arrived a little later that morning. I finally got to my desk and I took out my math book, the spiral notebook, and my freshly sharpened pencil. There was always a math assignment on the board as we arrived in the classroom. I was on the last math problem when I looked up at the clock. Laura had been in the principal's office over thirty minutes. Just as I was about to close my math book, I could see Laura just outside the classroom door. I could tell she had been crying. We have been friends for a very long time. I know when Laura pats her cheeks, she has been crying. My heart cried too as I watched her put on her smile for the rest of the class.

2 CHAPTER

When I am not watching the snow floating around outside the smudged window, I watch Mark sitting at his desk attempting to pay attention to Mr. Zim. I know I should be paying attention too, but it is so hard when I keep thinking of Laura. Seeing Mark, Alan and Joe doesn't help me either. Laura's desk is empty today. She didn't call me to tell me she that she wasn't going to be in school today. She doesn't seem herself lately. She usually loves to gossip about all the other girls in our class. She critiques the boys, too. For about three months she has just been very sad. She is polite to her friends and she does laugh at all our jokes. But I know she is keeping something a secret.

All of a sudden I heard Mr. Zim asking a question about probability. And his face was looking directly into mine. “Huh”, I answered. My face turned red like the geranium on Mr. Zim’s desk. I was mortified. The other kids were laughing at me. Even Mark.

Mr.Zim growled, “See me after school today, Emily.”

The end of the school day couldn’t come fast enough for me. I wanted to get this meeting over with so I could go home and call Laura. I wonder if she would tell me the truth. The boys were getting their belongings out of their lockers in the back of our room. The girls were waiting anxiously for Mr. Zim to give them a nod to get their belongings. I didn’t bother moving. I placed my head on my books that were on top of my desk. I felt like drifting off to sleep but I knew that would be impossible since I was going to get in trouble any minute.

Then I heard his booming voice as he stood behind his desk. “Emily, why haven’t you been paying attention in class lately? You know your parents expect me to contact them when your grades start slipping again. I am afraid I will have to schedule a meeting with them, tomorrow. ”

“Please don’t do that Mr. Zim. I know I haven’t been doing my best lately, but I have been worried about Laura. Do you know what’s going on with her?”

Mr. Zim responded, “I can’t tell you anything about Laura, but you can call her yourself, you know. She may not be able to share everything with you but I am sure she will appreciate your concern. Then maybe you can get your head back into your schoolwork. I will give you one more week to get yourself together and if things do not improve I will be calling your parents. Looks like ‘Disney’ may not be an option this year.”

I slowly got up and hoped Mr. Zim wouldn't see the drawings I made of Mark. I quickly grabbed them from the top of my books and put them in a worn-out folder. I told Mr. Zim I was going to go to 'Disney' this year because I wanted to make my parents proud of me. They were really great parents sometimes. They scolded me for eating so much junk food sometimes but basically they treated me fairly.

I was zipping up my very used winter coat and suddenly stopped because the zipper got stuck. I made it half way up to my neck but I didn't care. I wanted to hurry home. I was on a mission. Mr. Zim smiled at me and waved his hand as if to say he really didn't enjoy reprimanding me. I know he was only doing it to help me. Feeling ashamed I whispered, "Good Bye, Mr. Zim."

I walked home as swiftly as possible. It was

difficult trudging up and down the snow banks. People don't shovel their sidewalks so I had to walk in the road or plow through the snow. I made it home by four o'clock. Mom was in the living room playing golf on the Wii that my uncle gave to us. Something was baking in the oven. I smelled lemon and orange. It smelled fresh, like eating an orange just plucked from the tree. I hoped that mom made my favorite cake, orange supreme with lemon frosting. I didn't want to take time to check. So I threw my books and half-zipped coat on the bottom step. I ran upstairs to my bedroom shouting over the Wii. "Mom, I'm home."

I jumped on the bed kicking off my boots. I tracked wet, dirty snow all the way to my bedroom. I hoped it would dry before mom saw it. Then I could just sweep it up. The phone was on my freshly painted blue dresser. I grabbed it and dialed Laura's number.

Someone answered the phone with a very gruff voice. I never heard it before. I timidly asked if Laura was there.

The man said, "I'm sorry she cannot come to the phone right now."

"Thanks", I responded. Well that was that. I still don't know what's going on with Laura. I will just hope that she comes to school tomorrow.

I cleaned up the dried snow and went into the kitchen where my mom had spread the lemon frosting artistically on the orange cake. She handed me the spatula to lick the remaining frosting. It was the best part of my day.

3 CHAPTER

Christina jumped in front of Laura and me in the lunch line. Laura came back to school after being absent three days. I was a happier person when she was around. Christina was always a bit loud and overbearing. She had placed earphones in her ears and began dancing to a silent beat all the way to the cafeteria. Without skipping a beat she boogied through the lunch line and grabbed her choices for the day. She loved dunkers. They are like chicken fingers that can be dunked into red sauce. Most of the time, Christina wore the red sauce on her face. I tried telling her a couple times to use her napkin but she just ignored me and sang out loud to music only she heard.

I quietly asked the lunch lady at the counter, if I could please have some dunkers too. As she placed them on my tray, I told her to keep the red sauce. I was really hungry. My mom made a nutritious lunch for me but I knew I was going to need something more to get me through science class today. I had to search in the bottom of my pocket to find the extra money I needed to pay for those dunkers. I knew I was a little overweight but my real friends never made fun of me. They always asked me what was in my lunch bag. Most of the time they wanted me to share my lunch with them. They loved the cut up pieces of juicy fruit my mom put in plastic containers. Christina always ate my apple and Laura ate the watermelon chunks.

Laura was the last of our group to go through the lunch line. She didn't get very much to eat but I planned for her to eat my watermelon, especially today. I made sure there were plenty of juicy pieces in the pink container. It was so cool to have her back to school today. Laura came over to the table hesitantly. She didn't sit down and we could tell she was going to tell us something.

Finally, she stammered."I'm going to eat with the principal today". We looked at each other with surprised gazes on our faces. Who in their right mind would want to eat with the principal? None of us knew what to say to Laura.

As Laura started out of the cafeteria door, Christina jumped up with the earphones still attached to her head. She shouted, "Hey, we want to eat with you in the principal's office. C'mon, Emily."

"I guess it would be OK," Laura commented. "I'm sure Mrs. Lutnam wouldn't mind."

I quickly snapped the lids on the containers of grapes, watermelon, and apple slices my mom had lovingly prepared for me. I never have been to the principal's office. I used to steal a peek into her office whenever I was in the main office. I am not sure what I was expecting to find. I had heard about the switches and paddles that some principals used in the olden days. But they wouldn't use them today...would they?

We walked very slowly and cautiously into the main office together. That is, all of us except for Laura. She comfortably waltzed into the main office announcing to Ms Rapp, the secretary, that she had an appointment with Mrs. Lutnam. We watched Ms Rapp smile at Laura, get up from her desk, walk over to the principal's door and signal for all of us to enter. I expected Mrs. Lutnam to ask us to come back another time when she could plan for all of us. I started to turn around and return to the loud cafeteria filled with the aroma of dunkers.

"Oh my goodness, I have all these guests for lunch today? Come right in. Ms Rapp, would you bring us an extra chair, please?" She sounded so excited to see all of us. She sat right down at her round table with us and began to eat her lunch. She ate only an orange and sipped some strong smelling black coffee while she involved us in conversation. She had a way of getting us to spill our guts while we were in there. She was so easy to talk with. She listened as if our stories were the best in the world. We soon learned that she was a great friend and that we could go to her for anything.

Laura spent many mornings in Mrs. Lutnam's office after that first lunch outing we had all together. We all wondered what was cooking up in there. Laura was very closemouthed about it and we let her be that way for awhile. Except for that one day in February.

4 CHAPTER

The kickball rushed by my face. I was quietly sitting on the sideline with Christina and Laura in gym class. I looked in the direction of the sailing ball and there was Alan, the new boy, waiting to pounce on the foul ball. He took a leap hoping to stop it from bouncing into a group of other students. He crashed down on the gym floor as he hugged the ball. There he was, wiped out and everyone jumped to their feet waiting to see if Alan was going to get up by himself. Mr.Merl, our gym teacher, ran over to him. We were quietly waiting for Mr. Merl to speak.

Alan had dark hair that he obviously had trimmed on a regular basis. It flipped up in front and it always looked wet because of something he put on his hair. It really made him look cool. He was a rather quiet kid, but when his face spread to reveal his smile it made all of us girls melt. He always wore Nike clothes as if he wanted everyone to know he was not poor.

Suddenly, Alan rolled over and we caught a glimpse of that huge smile that was pasted on his face. He was quite pleased that he had indeed caught the kickball. Mark came running over to see if Alan was hurt and when he saw that smile, he retorted, "Great catch."

Of course, no one apologized for the ball almost knocking my head off. We three girls struggled to get up after sitting on the gym floor for thirty minutes. We walked over to Mr. Merl . We were going to complain about the ball, but we really wanted to get closer to Mark, Alan and Joe.

Mark's curly blonde hair and blue eyes sent a

charge straight to me. He was the class clown and always got into trouble. Just this morning in science class Mark decided to use Mr. Zim's leftover coffee for our experiment. Our group was scheduled to present information on geothermal energy so we decided to build a volcano that would erupt during our presentation. Hundreds of kids had done this experiment before us so we figured there would be no problems. Well, our volcano did erupt but something must have been in that coffee that magnified its energy tenfold! Everyone in the first two rows of seats, including Mr. Zim who was sitting at my desk, got plastered with the brown colored gook. Little rivers of brown were slowly dripping from Amy's horrified face onto her desk. John's new DARE shirt now fashioned a huge brown spot centered on his back. Lily's socks were drenched as she dangled them in front of the class.

Mr. Zim stood up very slowly. Mark, Gretta and I stood in the front of the classroom, relieved that the volcano erupted on the side facing the class and not us. We waited for Mr. Zim to scold us in front of our friends. It was Mark's fault. He never even asked us if we agreed to the coffee. But we were his friends and I knew that we were all going to pay for this blunder. None of us would dare squeal on Mark. As Mr. Zim stood, in horror we could see the huge wet spot right in the crotch of his khaki pants. His face was very red. The geranium on his desk looked rather pale compared to his face. He shook the front of his pants with the tips of his fingers. Mark grabbed my hand while we waited for our punishment. As he realized what he was doing, he quickly released my hand and gave me a terrifying look.

"It seems to me that something went wrong

with this experiment and that we have some very irresponsible students in our classroom who owe us an apology." As Mr. Zim stated this, he surveyed the class. We noticed his facial expression slowly changed from serious to a guarded smirk. But when he saw Amy's dripping face and Lily's now beige socks, dancing in the air as Lily tried to dry them, his sense of humor overpowered him. He let out the most robust laugh I have ever heard. Once the class witnessed his reaction, everyone started roaring with laughter. Alan even rolled on the floor.

Suddenly, Alan shot to his seat as if the principal were watching. I turned toward the door and she WAS . Mrs. Lutnam did not look happy.

She demanded, "Mr. Zim, meet me in my office during your lunchtime tomorrow."

He calmly replied, “Okay, I’ll be there.” He did not seem to be annoyed or afraid of her. We feared that Mr. Zim was going to be in real trouble. So, a few of us decided to talk about it after lunch during recess.

5 CHAPTER

It was Laura, Christina, Mark, Alan and I who finally did meet after school to talk about Mr. Zim getting in trouble with the principal. We felt really badly because it was Mark's fault. So we decided to make an appointment with Mrs. Lutnam during our lunch time the next day. We wanted to explain that it wasn't Mr. Zim who caused the disaster in the classroom.

Mark had never been in the principal's office before. We had seen Alan in there a few times but we didn't know why he was in there. He just wasn't the type of kid who got in trouble. But we just forgot about it and never asked him any questions.

It was Tuesday, the next day. It was our favorite day because Mr. Zim always allowed us to have study hall at the end of the day on Tuesdays, instead of listening to a social studies lesson. We really did do our homework in study hall, too. The best part was that we could sit with our friends and help each other. Of course, I always wanted to be next to Christina. We noticed Mark always worked with Alan. Alan was the smartest kid I have ever known.

The clock was ticking very slowly. I watched it while Mr. Zim demonstrated a science experiment in the front of the class. He managed to get an egg inside a jar that had an opening smaller than the egg. I wasn't really listening so I have no clue how that happened. Finally one last click and the big hand of the clock was smack on the 12. I thought, "Hurry up, Mr. Zim. Mrs. Lutnam will be waiting for us." At 12:03 Mr. Zim finally called us up to get in line for lunch. I was first in line. Christina had her earphones already in her ears as she filed in behind me. Laura squeezed in between the boys and us.

We waited for Alan and Mark to go through the lunch line before we could all go the main office together. Tuesday was always spaghetti day. I hoped Mrs. Lutnam would like the tangy smell of the boys' lunches. She seemed to be a nice person the last time I was in her office.

The boys joined us in the hall where we waited for them. Mark commented, "Let's hurry and tell the old bag our story and then we can finish our lunch in the cafeteria with the other kids." We all gave Mark a dirty look and proceeded to announce to Ms Rapp that we were here for our appointment.

The other secretary, Mrs.Till, said to Ms Rapp, "Don't let them go in there yet. Mrs. Lutnam has a visitor in there."

I thought, "Oh, no. We won't have enough time to explain everything to Mrs. Lutnam."

At that moment, Mrs. Lutnam opened her door to let us know that she would be just one moment. We could see a small boy in her rocking chair holding a big book on his lap. In a very few seconds the kindergartener opened the door slowly and proceeded into the main office. Mrs. Lutnam was behind him wearing a pleasant smile. The big book was positioned under the boy's arm with one hand holding the book and the other holding a brand new unsharpened pencil with the words, "Great job," written on it.

"Ms Rapp, who are all these students?" Before Ms Rapp could answer Mrs. Lutnam waved her arm at us motioning for us to enter her office. She made room around her table for all of us to sit. She even let me sit in her desk chair that was on rollers and could go up and down too. There was a lever under the chair that controlled the up and down. She sat in an old chair that she dragged to the table. There were stuffed bears carefully placed on her couch in her office. I was mesmerized by one that had red hearts all over it.

Before we began to chat, she shared with us that she had been cleaning out her desk and had found some very old looking keys. She had no idea what the keys opened. She dropped the keys in the middle of the table. We all admired them. One of them had a worn tassel on it. The others had an emblem on them but it was very hard to decipher the imprint. Mark picked up the keys and he was examining them. He seemed very interested in the whole idea of the mystery keys.

Mrs. Lutnam interrupted our thoughts by asking us why we had made the appointment to see her. We were so involved in the keys we practically forgot about

Mr. Zim.

At last, Christina interjected, "We feel so badly about Mr. Zim getting in trouble with you the other day. It was our fault that we were all laughing uncontrollably."

She responded quickly, "Mr. Zim is not in trouble with me. He told me all about the experiment. I laughed too when I heard all about it. And Mark, you and your partners should discuss plans before you continue with a group project. This time no one got hurt, but someone could have. Think before you act." Then Mrs. Lutnam cheerfully reminded us that she was not able to share personal matters.

With a quizzical look on my face, I asked, "Then why is Mr. Zim going to have a substitute for a few weeks?"

Something must be wrong. He is never out of school. I wonder if we could ask the secretaries where he is. I know they know everything that goes on in this school. Sometimes they keep secrets from Mrs. Lutnam. That's what my mom says anyway.

When Laura rubbed the key with the tassel, Mrs. Lutnam whispered to us that she found out that there were very old pieces of furniture in the basement of the school. Maybe the keys belonged to one of the old desks. She never did answer my question about the substitute for Mr. Zim.

6 CHAPTER

February started with a frosty blizzard. It lasted five days. School was canceled for six days in all. We had a grand vacation. Not only did I start an ant farm, I changed my bedroom furniture around. I wanted to be sure that the ants had plenty of sunlight. So I pushed my dresser under the window. Then I placed the ant farm in the middle of my old, tarnished dresser. My bed was next to the dresser now and I could view the sky during the silent nights as everyone slept. Looking outside my small uncovered window at the starry sky, I thought of my friends at school. I missed being with them and now we were all anxious for Mrs. Lutnam to tell us more about the keys. I couldn't wait for school to begin tomorrow.

My eyes began to feel very droopy. I wanted to

look at the stars a little longer, but as I was staring at them just before I fell asleep, I noticed the clouds taking the shape of a lighthouse. They floated by quickly and the twinkle at the top of the lighthouse appeared to be a red diamond shaped figure. The shape vanished as quickly as it formed. My eyes finally closed and I slumbered off wondering what I would wear to school tomorrow.

The phone woke me up way too early. It was only 7:00 a.m. and I was still lying on my back facing toward the window. I remembered that I wanted to wear my red sweater with the silver threads weaved through it horizontally. Of course, I would wear my jeans and sneakers. My winter coat was still half way zipped up since November. I couldn't get it unstuck so I have just been wearing it that way. When it got really cold I held my coat together so I didn't freeze.

I ran over to check my ant farm. So far, they had been busily carving tunnels.

My mom hollered to me from the kitchen, "Emily, the phone is for you. It sounds like Laura." I moved so quickly I stumbled over my books that were all over the floor.

"Coming," I shouted. I finally got to the phone. I greeted Laura with, "Hey, what's up?" Laura told me that she would not be in school for a while. I asked her why and she told me that she was moving to her grandparents' home in Ohio. I was stunned. We have been together since kindergarten. How was I going to manage without Laura? After I hung up the phone, I sat on my bed slowly slinking onto the floor where I just sat and stared at the wall.

"Emily, breakfast has been ready for five minutes.

Hurry down," my mother demanded while she darted past the stairway. A couple more minutes went by and I heard my mother's heels striking the stairs as she climbed to my room. "What is going on? Are you sick?" my mother asked. "Get up off the floor and tell me what is wrong."

"Laura is moving. She will be gone for awhile in Ohio. What will I do without my best friend?" I whined. I crawled up to the top of my bed and sat there with my head down. My mother took my face gently in her hands and kissed my cheek. She reassured me that my other friends would help to fill the huge void that Laura's moving would cause. Her continuing words of comfort helped me to realize that "awhile" might not be so long.

I quickly wiggled into my jeans and lowered my sweater over my head without unbuttoning it. I finished getting ready for school, skipping breakfast. My mom gave me a ride to school as soon as I unleashed the dog and brought her in the front door. My mom gave me a reassuring smile as she waved to me through the car window. I wonder if anyone else knew about Laura.

7 CHAPTER

The winter chill usually sent us in the school foyer to wait for the morning bell. Two months had gone by since Laura left. This morning, as I moped along the snowpacked sidewalk, I noticed Christina, and Mark outside in conversation beneath Mrs. Lutnam's window. Their breath formed little puffs of clouds as they talked. I wondered if they were talking about Laura. My feet picked up speed as I approached them.

"Hey, I guess you've heard, huh." I said. They turned to look at me, but they had smiles on their faces. I wondered what information about Laura they had heard that made them so jovial.

Christina kept repeating, "That is so cool. That is so cool." She witnessed my perplexity and blurted out, "He's back!"

I could hear the muffled bell ringing inside the school. Christina, Mark and now Joe hustled into school before I could find out about Laura. I wondered if Christina had made a mistake when she said, “He” instead of “She.” I had to run to catch up with Christina. Our wet, snowy boots squeaked and squealed as we approached our classroom. Before I could ask Christina to explain what she told me outside, she pointed to the front of the class and restated, “He’s back.”

Indeed, he was. Mr. Zim stood behind his desk chitchatting with the students as they came into the classroom. We were certainly elated to see him. He had been gone for about six weeks, and we had had three different substitute teachers. Not many teachers could handle us like Mr. Zim. We wanted to behave for him because he really cared about us.

And then I saw Laura's empty desk and I began to feel empty inside, too. Obviously, no one seemed to care about Laura either. I felt myself getting angry at them but I was in school and decided to keep quiet. I finally looked up from my desk. Mr. Zim's desk looked strange. I couldn't figure out why. I examined every square inch to see if I could discover any changes. When my eyes moved to the tall, red geranium sitting on the side of the desk, I knew I was getting close to a discovery. The plant used to be in the center of the large, oak desk. Now there was another object there. I stood up from my desk and stepped closer to the center of the Mr. Zim's desk. I easily distinguished that now there were three pictures enclosed in a colorful, ceramic frame carefully arranged on Mr. Zim's desk.

At first I didn't understand. The pictures showed Mr. Zim, some lady and three different horses. One of the horses was adorned with a wreath of rainbow colored flowers. The other two had numbers on their saddle blankets that draped over their graceful bodies. The brown horse was number three and the ebony horse was wearing number ten. Suddenly, I remembered the time my grandfather took me to the horse races. I remembered that the winning horse always had a picture taken with the owners. A wreath of flowers was always placed around the winning horse's neck, too.

So that was it. Mr. Zim and that lady must have owned the horses in the pictures. One of them indeed won a race. But it was wintertime. Where do horses run in the winter? I decided I would ask Mr. Zim when I had time.

Well, it turned out that I didn't need to find time to ask Mr. Zim. He shared the story of the pictures with the whole class. He took us back to the day when we were all laughing hysterically and Mrs. Lutnam surprised us and came into the room. When she demanded that he come to her room the next day during his lunch time, she wasn't going to reprimand him. She needed to talk to him about the days that he requested for a leave. He and his wife needed to go to Tampa, Florida where their horses were scheduled to run. Mr. Zim told us he needed special permission from the superintendent and Mrs. Lutnam to go to Florida.

Mark raised his hand and when Mr. Zim called on him to respond, Mark asked, "Do you have to get a sub again this year?"

"Nope," replied Mr. Zim.

"Great," Mark chuckled. "Those substitute teachers sucked."

I felt a little bit better now that Mr. Zim was back. I still missed Laura. She had been gone for two months now.

8 CHAPTER

Walking back to the classroom from gym class, Christina, Mark, Alan and I were talking about our lunch with Mrs. Lutnam earlier in the year. Alan suggested that it would be cool to explore the basement to see if those keys fit into any of those desks. "You know, I heard that our school was built on top of a cemetery. Maybe we will find skeletons down there," Alan remarked. "The Mohawk tribe had a burial ground near here. We studied that in fourth grade."

Mark offered his opinion and stated, "Yeah. I heard that too. But I also heard that it was a garbage dump after that. I hope we don't run into any rotten garbage. I couldn't stand it if we found old, used baby diapers or maggots scurrying all over the place."

"You are insane, Mark. After all these years I am

sure the diapers have disintegrated and the maggots are now fossils!" explained Christina.

I did not find their ideas very humorous. I for one am a little squeamish in damp, dark places. And with my allergies I am sure the mold would cause trouble for me. There is no way I can be quiet in places like that. I start sneezing and coughing.

It was getting close to our April break and no one had heard from Laura. We were all anxious for a break. We had been busy studying for tests and more tests. You could tell the teachers were all uptight about these tests too. We practiced and practiced taking sample tests. Maybe we did need something fun to do.

9 CHAPTER

Christina, Mark, Alan and I planned to meet at the school playground to hang out after school. I was a little late getting my books together for homework, so I took a shortcut through the gym. I heard a ball bouncing on the gym floor and off the backboard. So I stopped before I cut through the gym. I found Alan playing basketball by himself.

"Hey Alan, I thought we were supposed to meet outside," I shouted. He turned around quickly and gave me a quizzical look. "I think Christina and Mark are waiting for us. I thought we were going to talk about getting Laura to come for a visit during our spring break," I explained.

Alan just kept playing ball while he shouted back, "They canceled on us. So I decided to stay and play some basketball."

"Hey, can I play with you? I can play pretty good for a girl," I yelled.

All of a sudden Alan whirled around and pushed the ball toward me. I caught it and took that as a "yes" for an answer. I looked at the clock and reminded Alan that we were supposed to be out of the building by 4:00 p.m. at the latest. He smiled as he looked at me.

"I can stay as long as I want," he bragged.

"How come you get to stay," I whined.

He stopped bouncing the ball and walked over to me. He swore me to secrecy before he told me why he was allowed in the building after hours. He told me that Mrs. Lutnam was supervising him even though she was still working in her office. I thought that he had gotten into trouble and had to stay after school. But that seemed odd that he would be allowed to play in the gym if he were being punished.

He moved closer to me and whispered, “Mrs. Lutnam is my grandmother.”

“She’s what!” I screamed.

“Hey, keep quiet. I don’t want everyone to know. You know what some kids are like. They will make fun of me or something.”

“Well, I will keep it a secret. You know I won’t tell,” I whispered.

The clock was moving toward four and my mom was expecting me home by four. So I walked over to get my coat and books that I had dropped on the gym floor by the door. Alan was watching me so he picked up the ball that had been on the floor and waved good-by. I waved back and then I crossed my heart.

Alan told me later that he had decided to walk around the school until his grandmother was ready to go home. He stopped in the office to let her know. What he didn't tell her was that he wanted to explore downstairs in the basement. So he quietly and quickly opened the door to the basement and walked down the dimly lit stairs. He saw old desks piled on top of one another and he spotted old teachers' desks over in the corner. Boxes and boxes of books were everywhere. He started to look through one of the boxes and heard jingling. He knelt down quickly behind the old desks. He didn't want anyone to find him snooping around. While he was hiding there he could hear the jingling getting louder. He peeked through the desks and could see what was making the jingling sound. It looked like the janitor's keys. He could not tell which one of the janitors was in that room but he noticed a huge ring on his finger. It was decorated with a lighthouse with some jewel at the top.

Alan could feel his face getting hot. He hoped he could sneak out with no one noticing him. He waited until the jingling of the keys was completely gone. He slowly moved toward the stairs and stepped lightly on each step until finally he reached the door to the main floor of the school. Once he was in the main hallway he walked normally and wore a fake smile as if nothing happened. But he wondered why the janitor was down in that room. His grandmother said no one ever went in there.

Mrs. Lutnam was just locking the office door when Alan met her. She mumbled, "What a long day. I can't wait to go home and relax with a cup of tea."

Alan asked, "Can I carry some of your books for

you, Grandma? I don't have any homework tonight so I left my book bag in school."

"Sure, that would be a great help. By the way, what have you been doing since school let out?" she questioned.

Alan could feel his face getting warm again and his hands getting sweaty. But he decided to ask, "Grandma, does anyone ever need to go down in the basement at school for anything?"

She put her briefcase in the car and answered him quickly. "Of course not, Alan, there is nothing we need down there. No one is allowed down there without my permission."

Her answer made Alan uncomfortable. He knew someone was down there and they should not have been there. But he was down there too and he wasn't quite sure how his grandmother would react if she found out.

10 CHAPTER

Every night for about two weeks I looked in the newspaper to see how our sixth grade class did on the state tests. I flipped through the pages when something caught my eye. It looked like Laura's last name was in the paper. I turned the page back and scanned it. It wasn't on this page. I turned another one and my stomach churned. There it was. Her last name was in the headline on page six. As I looked closely at the name, I quickly realized that the article was about her father, Daniel Gardner. I began to shake wondering why her father's name would be in the paper. But there it was, "Daniel Gardner was sentenced to ten years in prison for child abuse and repeated domestic abuse." According to the article, her father had pushed her mom down the stairs. It wasn't specific about what he did to Laura, but it did say that the daughter tried to assist her mom when Mr. Gardner hit her with a board. That must have been why Laura was out of school for so long and why she had to go to Ohio to stay with her grandparents. Poor, Laura. What terrible secrets she had to hide all the time.

I knew the other kids had probably seen the article too. What could we have done to help Laura? She had been our friend since kindergarten. I waited to call Christina until later in the evening. My mom had prepared a delicious dinner, but I just couldn't eat. My mom and dad ate silently as they stared at me pushing my food around my plate. They knew that I had known for a long time that something was going on with Laura at home. I started to ask if I could be excused from the table but before I got the words out my mom had already motioned for me to go.

I lay on my bed looking out the window at the

sparkles in the sky. I wondered if Laura was looking up at the stars too. It made me feel sad to think that she was there without her friends, and without her mom. The tears trickled down my face when I heard the phone ring.

I heard my dad's voice saying, "She is in her room right now". Then he hollered up the steps to me. "Emily, Mark is on the phone."

I grabbed the phone in my room. I knew just what he was going to say. I wiped the warm tears from my face and sat on my bed still staring at the glazed sky. "Hey, Mark. What's up?"

Did you read the paper tonight?" Mark whispered.

"Yes, but I can't talk about it now. I'll see you in school tomorrow," I responded while trying to hold back tears. I was afraid if I kept talking that I would embarrass myself and start to choke on my words.

Well, at least Laura might be able to come home soon. Her mom probably needs her so much with everything going on. I asked my mom if she could find a way for me to call Laura. I knew she needed a friend now and I really missed her too.

I needed to talk to someone other than Mark so I decided to call Christina. I knew that she probably already knew about Laura's dad. I picked up the phone and started to dial her number. I had an unusual feeling as I was looking in the sky and saw a vision of a lighthouse with a ruby shining at the top. It was the same picture I had seen before. I wondered what it all meant and I decided to put the phone down and just stare out my window.

"Emily. Wake up. Wake up," my mother insisted.

"Christina and Mark are at the door. They want to talk with you." At first I thought I was dreaming and then I stood up and looked in the mirror. My hair was all on the left side of my head and my eyes looked like I was wearing a black mask. "What a mess," I thought. But I ran downstairs to find out what my friends wanted anyway.

11 CHAPTER

I found out later that Alan was at home with his family celebrating his great-grandmother's birthday. She was eighty-five that day and Alan loved it when the family got together. His uncles were comical, and his grandmother always treated him as if he were special. He told me his grandmother embarrassed him though because she was relentless about bragging about him and it made him blush.

Mark told me he called Alan to talk to him about Laura's family on his cell phone. Alan later told me his phone rang just as he was about to place a moist piece of chocolate cake in his mouth. The sweet, blue frosting just touched his mouth as he heard the phone singing, "Hey, Soul Sister." He dropped his fork on the plate as he answered his phone.

Alan continued telling me what happened at his grandmother's home that day. He answered his phone saying, "Hey, Mark. What's up?" He knew it was Mark because he recognized the number that came up on the face of his phone.

Mark replied with a strange sound in his voice. He told Alan to read the paper. Alan didn't know what to think. So he went directly into the living room to find the evening paper. He ended his phone call with Mark and it wasn't long before he found the article about Laura's father. His grandmother came in the room hoping not to disturb Alan. But she couldn't keep her concern quiet.

"Alan, I read about it too. I am sure Laura is in good hands at her grandparents' home. She will be with all her friends soon," she remarked in a gentle manner. She knew how sensitive Alan was. He knew that she understood his feelings. Alan understood more than anyone what it was like to have a family member's name in the newspaper, not because of their positive qualities, but because of their bad reputation.

I found out later, that a long time ago, Mrs. Lutnam's father, Mr. Ken Grove, was the principal of Grove Park School. Mr. Ken Grove had a brother, Tom, who always seemed to get into trouble. Tom Grove was a likeable guy but just couldn't keep away from the cops with all his shenanigans. One time he was a suspect in a robbery of a city bank. He worked at the bank as a custodian. The police could never find any evidence that it was he that stole the money. They were pretty sure it was Tom Grove but without any proof they could not keep him. So they had to release him from jail until more evidence could be found. Of course, all of this was printed in the paper making him look like the criminal that he really was.

Mr. Ken Grove was the principal of our school for over twenty years. Because of his popularity and his positive impact on the community, he was honored with his school being named after him. It was during this time that Tom, his brother, was getting noticed for his disservice to the community.

It was rumored that Ken Grove tried to keep the limelight off of his brother and hid the stolen money somewhere. But not many people believed that Ken would betray the community like that even if it was his brother. So, for years no one talked about this incident. And Alan certainly did not want anyone to know that Tom Grove was his great uncle.

12 CHAPTER

There they were standing at my front door waiting for me to say something. I knew they were upset and they probably wondered if I knew any details about Laura's situation. They stared at me as if I were some sort of alien.

"I just woke up," I remarked. "I don't always look like this! "

"OK, tell us everything you know. We are worried about Laura, too," Mark insisted. I invited them into the living room. Mark kept staring at me, and Christina had only one earphone in her ear. I asked them to sit down and told them that I would tell all that I knew about Laura.

As Christina jumped on the couch, I began talking. I explained that my mom assured me that I could invite

Laura here so that we could spend time with each other. Other than that I really did not know more than what they all read in the newspapers. I divulged that Laura did call me the day she had to leave but that she told me only that. The rest of what I knew was in the newspaper.

By the looks on their faces they seemed a little disappointed. I think they believed that Laura really did tell me more than that. I assured them that I felt horrible that they did not trust me. If I knew more I would tell them. Don't they know that about me?

I hoped they would leave soon. I wasn't in the mood to talk to them. I wanted to be alone or with Laura. She was the one friend who really knew me and understood me. I could tell her anything and she would keep it to herself...always. Like the time I told her that I had a crush on Mark. I wanted him to notice me so much, but when he did, it was because he wanted to get to know Laura even more. He used me for that. Laura knew that about Mark and was always mad at him.

I couldn't wait for spring break to get here. We were all a little stressed out for different reasons. My grades had improved, thanks to Christina. I had hoped for the trip to Disney this summer. My parents were very proud of me. I had one more grading period to get on the honor roll to see our deal come through. I wanted to ask Laura to come with us to Disney, but we had to wait to see what was going on in her life, too.

Christina picked her purse up from the floor and placed it on her shoulder. She remarked, "Well, we found out all we could. It's time to go." Mark followed her lead and began walking toward the door. I waved good-by to them as they walked down the front steps.

I ran up to my room and watched the ants scurry around in their farm doing all the necessary chores to survive. Sometimes I wished I was an ant. Life seemed so simple in there. But of course, they don't know about my mother's famous orange cake with lemon frosting. And I bet they wouldn't enjoy Disney either.

13 CHAPTER

Spring break was in two days. All of us were excited for a time away from the demanding teachers and relentless schedules. We would get together with our friends and have a great time. Laura was going to visit me. My mom had arranged for her to stay with us for a few days. My mom always did thoughtful things for me. I couldn't wait!

Finally, Tuesday was here, the day Laura was coming. Mark, Christina, Alan and I were so excited to see our good friend Laura again. We planned to meet at my house to share our favorite pepperoni pizza and root beer floats while we waited for Laura. Mark arrived first and never sat down the whole time. He wandered all over the living room like a caged monkey. Alan sat in a chair by himself and read the newspaper. He seemed in an odd mood. We all knew that he was shy, but he usually talked with us. Christina and I never stopped chattering. We sounded like a nest of newly hatched birds looking for their mother.

Mark peered out the window and suddenly reported, “She’s here.” We all jumped up and ran to the front door. Laura looked like the day we last saw her in school. The thing I noticed was her eyes. They were filled with sorrow even though her mouth turned up in a smile.

We shared food and fun. Finally, Alan spoke. “I have an idea. I think we should go exploring in the basement of the school while Laura is here.”

“We can’t do that. We would get into big trouble with Mrs. Lutnam and ....how would we get the keys to the building?” asked Christina.

“Since all of you now know that the principal is my

grandmother, I think I can figure out a way to get the keys and get in the school without anyone knowing. We want Laura to be with us....right?" Alan argued.

Everyone looked at each other and sheepishly answered, "Right."

By the way everyone else was looking at one another, I figured that they had no idea what Alan was talking about. I was glad that I had kept Alan's secret. Alan focused on Christina and Mark and finally hinted, "Why do you think I was in the office so much? You know I don't get into trouble at school. I was just visiting my grandmother."

Laura, Mark and Christina turned their heads toward me and I confessed, "Yes, I knew about it, but Alan swore me to secrecy! All right, let's talk about your stupid idea, Alan. Why would we want to risk getting into trouble?" I questioned.

"Listen. I was in the basement snooping around one day, and I noticed someone was already down there. My grandmother said that no one should be down there without her permission. So I know this person was breaking the rules. We need to find out who it is and tell my grandmother about it. Laura is only here a few days. So we have to do it now!" he pleaded.

Mark had a big grin on his face. And Christina was looking at me waiting for my reaction. I decided that Laura could use a distraction in her life and we really wanted to try to find out about that person who was in the basement so we could tell Mrs. Lutnam.

It was like Alan could read my mind. So he said, "OK, let's meet tomorrow at my grandmother's house.

As everyone left, I felt my heart pounding in my chest and in my throat. I never got in trouble like other kids. I felt my skin turn red and sweaty all over. Laura and I ran upstairs to my room. Laura was getting ready for bed in the bathroom and I wanted to crawl into bed and hide under the covers. Laura probably felt like that her whole life before her dad went to prison.

Laura pushed the door open slowly. She had only her nightgown on as she slid into bed. I could see the scars on her back protruding through the sheer material. She had been through so much. My heart flipped as I tried to think about our upcoming crime. I needed to help Laura heal from all her hurts. I decided I needed to do this for her. She needed a huge distraction from her life. I decided that if we all get suspended from school she would not feel so alone in her misery. I was in!

14 CHAPTER

The telephone rang and rang. Was I dreaming or was it for real? Finally I felt a gentle nudge from Laura. She explained, "The phone...aren't you going to answer it?' I rolled over and saw that Laura had showered, dressed and was ready for the day. She had a journal in her hand. It looked as if she had been writing in it waiting for me to wake up. I quickly scanned the open page and I noticed that my name was in there.

"Uh, Hello. This is Emily. Of course, we are both still in. OK. We will meet you at 2:00." I immediately felt hot and sweaty again. I knew my face turned red, too.

"Emily, are you okay?" Laura asked.

"Yes, but we have to figure out a story to tell my parents. I told Mark and Alan that we would meet them at 2:00 today at Alan's grandmother's house. We have to keep her occupied while Alan looks for the keys to the school and then goes to get them copied. Do you think we can come up with a believable story?" I wondered out loud.

Laura answered quickly, "I am good at lying, Emily. I have had to do it most of my life. I will come up with a most believable story for your parents. But we have to rehearse it so we are both on the same page. Give me a minute to write it down."

While Laura contemplated our alibi, I decided to get showered and dressed. I was all put together when I heard Laura say, "Emily, come on. We have to go over this before we go down for breakfast." I hurried into my bedroom and Laura's facial expression told me she really enjoyed this whole escapade.

I grabbed the script from Laura and read it over carefully. "Okay, I know all the details, Laura. I am ready to tell my parents our great story. C'mon let's go downstairs. I am starving," I replied.

Laura and I sat down at the breakfast table. My parents drank freshly brewed coffee behind yesterday's newspapers. I could smell the aroma of freshly ground coffee beans. They usually drink three cups before they begin their daily chores. I glanced at the coffee pot to try to decipher how many cups had been already consumed. It appeared that they are on their last cup. Laura and I had little time to present our charade. I looked at Laura. She returned a stare. I began.

"Mom, Laura and I are going to visit Mrs. Lutnam today. She asked if we could come over for lunch so she could catch up with Laura. She said she had a lot to do today and wondered if we could stop by at two. We will probably be a couple hours. We don't want to eat and run. So Laura and I will see you at dinner. Is that Okay?" I held my breath.

Laura and I were afraid to look at each other. My mother's answer was, "Who called this morning?" I remember rehearsing this with Laura. "Alan called. He stayed at his grandmother's last night and he was the one who gave us the message from his grandmother, Mrs. Lutnam." Both my parents moved the newspapers ever so slightly to get a view of me.

"Mrs. Lutnam is Alan's grandmother?" my father retorted. "When did you find this out?"

"Well, he just told everybody the other day. We knew there had to be something going on between them because Alan was always in the principal's office and we knew he didn't get in trouble. I guess he figured everybody would find out eventually anyhow, so he just told us." I answered.

I still anxiously waited for the response to the lunch invitation. I looked at my mother. She looked up at me and said, "What"?

I replied, "So, Mom, can we go to lunch at Mrs. Lutnam's?"

She looked back at the newspaper and muttered "Of course".

Wow, that seemed really simple. Was I worried for nothing?

15 CHAPTER

Laura and I jumped on my bike. She rode on the seat while I pedaled. My legs ached with each rotation. It was harder and harder to push even though we were on level ground. Laura offered to take a turn doing the pedaling and I immediately agreed. She seemed to have no trouble at all moving through the loose graveled trail to Mrs. Lutnam's house. We were almost there and we saw Alan and Mark outside playing hoops. Alan was taller than Mark and he was making basket over basket. Up on the porch we saw Christina. She stood up when she saw Laura and me approaching the driveway.

Christina pulled the wires out of her ears and exclaimed, "Hey, we were hoping you would be here pretty soon. Alan's grandmother is still upstairs getting ready to go shopping. We have to hurry to find the keys to the school before she comes downstairs. "

I didn't hear the basketball bouncing any more. The boys had started toward the porch when all of us heard a scream coming from the bedroom. Alan ran inside and up the stairs. His grandmother had fallen and hurt her arm. She was lying on the floor trying to get up when Alan said," Grandma, just stay there. I will get some help." We saw him running to the phone. We heard him say, "Hurry, please. She seems to be in a lot of pain."

Mark said, "Well, guys, I am not sure what we will do now. We will have to let Alan make the calls." Mark went to talk with Alan and Alan put his fingers to his lips as if to say, "This is not the time to talk about it." Mark backed off and sat on the steps of the porch. We all joined him and began to talk about school and everything that happened that Laura should know about. After all, she was going to come back and she needed to know. Joe had moved away. His father was laid off and they went to New Jersey to find work for him. Joe didn't care though. He could make friends anywhere.

We could hear the crunching of the gravel as a car approached. It was Alan's mom. She had come to take Mrs. Lutnam, her mother, to the emergency room. Alan helped his grandmother get in the car and gave her a kiss good-bye. He turned to look at us. We were quiet with apprehension and wonderment. "Is Alan still going through with the plans?" we were all thinking.

Alan's expression changed from concern to a look of deviousness. Our stoic faces relaxed to confident grins. We knew he would come through. We stood up and prepared for our orders. Alan stated, "Now that she is out of the house, it will be really easy to get the keys. Let's go inside." We all followed Alan as he went to the brown, antique hutch. He reached into the bottom drawer and opened a tin box. That's when I began to feel sick to my stomach. It just didn't feel right. My mom always told me that if something didn't feel right then it probably isn't. I didn't know what to do or say. I had already committed to my friends. I just couldn't back out now. I looked at Laura for some sign that she felt uncomfortable but her eyes were lit up like our Christmas lights. She was really enjoying this. I knew I was going to pay for this in some way.

The keys were jingling in Alan's hand. He told us that he and Mark were going to the hardware store to get another set of keys made for us. We were supposed to wait here and begin making plans for our escapade.

We returned to the top step of the porch and Christina started the conversation by asking what day would be the best for all of us to get together. We decided it would have to be on the week-end when no one would be using the school building. Sunday was it. We would tell our parents we were going to church with Laura and then would be spending time with her before she had to go back home. Of course I had to tell my parents that we were at Christina's house.

Alan and Mark returned and we shared the plans we had made. Alan put the original keys back. When he came back out on the porch, they agreed with what we had planned but mentioned that there were many more details that needed to be determined. They resumed playing basketball and we got back on my bike and headed home. We hollered to Mark, Alan and Christina still on the porch. "Good-bye. See you

Sunday."

16 CHAPTER

Okay. This was my last chance to get out of this mess. It was Saturday when Laura, Christina, Mark, Alan and I met in the morning. We decided on all the final details for our exploring expedition tomorrow. They appointed me the job of "lookout person". So, I am supposed to guard the door to make sure I let them know if someone else comes into the building. I was supposed to have a flashlight and blink it three times toward the basement window if someone was coming. Everyone else got their duties assigned too. Laura and I left to go back to my house.

After picking at dinner Laura and I went to bed. My heart was pounding. I could not sleep. I looked over at Laura and she seemed to be sleeping fine. I guess if you have gone through her life, you would have to learn to go to sleep quickly so you could forget about everything. But I couldn't sleep. I imagined my parents' faces and I didn't want to disappoint them. But I also saw my friends' faces and I knew they were counting on me, too. The sweat was dripping from my forehead and I had to kick off the heavy covers. Okay, I guess I had gone too far. There was no turning back now. Maybe we would never get caught anyway. And what were we really doing that was wrong? Alan is the one who took the keys from his grandmother's house.

I must have fallen asleep because I awoke when I heard the water running in the bathroom next to my room. Laura's bed was empty. I turned to look at the clock. It was 9:00 a.m. Church began at 10:00 a.m. so I thought I had better get up too. We had to make my parents believe we really were going to church. So I had to wear my nicer jeans and top. I still didn't feel right about this.

Laura came into the room. She was dressed in her black jeans and her red sweater. She really looked nice. Her beautiful blonde hair shined as if it had been sprayed with sunshine. I looked at her and remarked, "I couldn't sleep last night. Could you?" She lifted her eyes to look at mine and answered, "I sure did and I am ready for today! I really need this. My life has been so horrible up to now. I want some fun."

"Great. Now I felt like I really needed to do this for Laura. So this was going to be okay, right?"

We both went down to breakfast together. My parents were in their bedroom. My mom hollered down. "Go ahead and get what you want to eat. Dad and I are going to read the paper in bed this morning. We will see you after you go to church and then to Christina's."

I couldn't eat. I drank some milk but that was it. Laura ate some of the crunchy Cheerios with bananas decorating the top of the bowl. It was 9:45 a.m. We needed to leave soon. We put the dishes in the sink and grabbed our jackets. We opened the door and I yelled up the stairs, "See you later, Mom."

We were on our way to Christina's when I remembered that we were supposed to stop at Mark's house so I could get the flashlight. I turned the bike in the direction of Mark's house and I heard Laura saying, "Look up at the sky. The clouds are shaped like a lighthouse. If you really look hard you can make out something shiny on top of the lighthouse too."

Oh, no. What did that mean? It's the same picture I have seen out my window. Before I could dwell on it any longer we were already at Mark's house. He was outside emptying the garbage bagged up in a dark green plastic bag. He waved to us as we got closer and then he put his hand over his mouth, as if to tell us he forgot something.

"Hey. Were you guys supposed to come here this morning?" And then as quickly as Mark uttered the words, his face was beaming with a smile.

"You are a jerk", I said. "I am already a nervous wreck. Don't make it any worse with your teasing!"

"Wait a minute. I'll go get the flashlight. Christina said we could all meet at her house to go over all the plans before we go over to the school. We have to wait until it is dark anyway. So we can play some games and maybe shoot some hoops too", Mark rambled on.

We were on our way to Christina's house. Just as we were approaching her block, we noticed that Alan was pedaling his bike toward her house, too. Everyone was waving, except for me. I just wasn't as excited as they all were about this whole thing. As we got to her house, Christina came out on the porch and told us to put our bikes on the driveway. She told us her parents were going to be home all day and that they planned to fix us pizza for lunch. We went inside and downstairs to the basement. It didn't look like a basement. The floors were carpeted and there was really nice leather furniture all around. There were shelves full of games and CDs. A wooden bar was situated in a corner with cups and paper plates stacked on the top. It was warm and pleasant down there. I liked the smell, too. It reminded me of the lavender bushes outside my grandmother's house that filled the air with a sweet, soothing aroma.

We had so much fun eating, drinking and playing games that I just about forgot why we had planned to meet there. But as the sun was disappearing from the sky, I was reminded of the flashlight. And all our plans were bouncing around in my head.

Alan began. "Well, it's almost time. I have the keys. Does everyone have what they need and know what to do?"

The rest of us stood up. I held the flashlight close to my body. Mark gave all of us the signal to begin our master plan. We told Christina's parents good bye, explaining that we were going to my house as it was Laura's last night here with all of us. But we knew we were not going to my house. I knew we were going to pay for this escapade somehow.

17 CHAPTER

The sun had fallen. We had to time it just right so we didn't arrive at school when someone could notice us. We looked at each other as we sat on the porch in front of Christina's house. We jumped on our bikes and headed toward the Grove Park School. Alan was in the lead. Mark followed behind Alan and then the girls trailed behind Mark. I had Laura on my bike and I struggled to keep up with everyone.

As soon as we arrived at school, we hid our bikes in the bushes in the back. Alan took the duplicate keys and opened the door leading to the basement. We hurried into the building and immediately ventured up to Mrs. Lutnam's office to get the old keys she had shown us before; the day we all had lunch with her. Then we ran down the stairs to the basement. I wasn't going to stay alone to guard the door. It was spooky in this building at night. Even though there were security lights on, it gave us an eerie feeling to be in here.

We followed Alan to the back door that was hidden behind huge boilers. He opened it slowly and going down the steps we found very old desks and chairs piled on top of each other. There were old musty boxes lined up against the wall. Laura was the first one to open the boxes while Christina held the flashlight. There were yearbooks stacked in the boxes dating back to 1950. Laura and Christina were chatting about the funny hairdos that the girls wore then. I wanted to open one of the teachers' desks. The older desks had locks on them so we needed to see if the old keys that Alan got from the office would fit any of them. On one of the desks we saw a gold plate with the inscription, "Mr. Kenneth Grove".

"Alan, look, this is the old principal's desk", Laura exclaimed. "Let's try to open it."

Alan and Mark both came over to investigate. Sure enough they saw this gold plated inscription, too. Alan fumbled with the keys as he tried each one carefully in the keyhole. He had the key with the tassels, too. He tried that one. No luck!

Mark said, "Let's just break into the drawer. No one will ever know who did it. Someone has to know what is inside that desk."

I spoke up and said, "Forget it. I am sure someone must have cleaned out these desks before they put them in here."

As I shared my concerns Mark found another keyhole to the desk. This one was not visible unless you got under the desk and looked up. There it was shining from the flashlights that each of us held and now pointed toward the keyhole. We were all stooped on our knees waiting for the tasseled key to turn and open this secret compartment. Alan turned it to the right. Nothing happened. Then he dropped the key and it made a clanging sound. We all gasped.

"Don't lose the key, Alan", we all softly told him.

While picking up the key, Alan noticed that the gold-plated nameplate was loose. He waved his hand over it, thinking, "My grandfather probably touched this many times." The nameplate moved with Alan's hand and looking at the desk from underneath, he noticed something. It was another keyhole. Quickly, Alan yanked the nameplate off and motioned for everyone to look. As we were getting in really close to where the nameplate had been, Alan placed the key in the hole.

He stopped. While turning around to say something, Mark grabbed the key and turned it quickly to the right. And there it was. We all heard the click.

Mark looked inside the tubular-shaped opening. He found a piece of paper that was rolled up and had writing on it. We all looked over his shoulder when Christina read it out loud. It read, 'Dear family and friends. If you have found this note you probably have discovered the secret I have to carry with me to the grave. Please know that I am not sorry for what I have to do. I am only sorry that I have to keep a secret from you. Love, Kenneth Grove.'

We were confused. None of us spoke for a minute or two. Alan rolled the note up and

placed it back where he had discovered it. He locked the desk and carefully placed the nameplate over the key hole. All eyes were on Alan.

"Some things are better left alone", Alan whispered.

"What do you mean? We all risked our reputations coming here and exploring. We wanted to find something special, didn't we?" I complained.

"Think about it. It must have been pretty serious if he had to keep it a secret. People loved him in this town. He must have had to protect his family from something they were better off not knowing. Do we really want to keep digging so we can discover what he was talking about?" Alan responded.

Christina remarked, "Okay. Okay. But can we keep exploring down here? We are here now, so let's do what we came for.....exploring!"

Everyone shook their heads in agreement. We all started to look in desk drawers that would open without a key. In one of the drawers way in the back, sticking out, was a white piece of paper. I pulled it out and began to read the paper. It was a note to a parent that never got finished. It started out saying, "Dear Ms Kraft, Your son was sent to the office today for not wearing the proper attire for the classroom. He sh....." That was as far as it got.

Laura ripped open another box and discovered copies of old unused report cards. Laura asked, "Hey guys, what is penmanship?" They each took a report card and studied it more carefully.

Mark inquired, "Who knows how to speak the language, Latin?" After a few chuckles, we heard footsteps and something jingling.

Alan waved his hand at us and put his fingers to his lips. Once he got our attention he finger-walked through the air. He pointed to the flashlights. We turned them off which left only the dim security lights on in the basement. We needed to hide - and quickly. The footsteps were getting louder. The footsteps stopped. I could hear rustling, like the sound plastic grocery bags make, but I didn't know where that noise was coming from. "Who would be here this time of night and what would they be doing here?" I wondered as I moved boxes and hid behind them.

Mark and Alan hid under Mr. Grove's desk. Laura was behind the chairs. The only light in the room was the light that filtered in through the fogged window in the door. It would be difficult to see us. Then, in an instant the door was opened to the room where we were hiding. I closed my eyes for a second and held my breath. We could see work boots moving around the room. There were keys dangling from a pocket. A hand reached down to the keys and selected one of them. What was happening?

I could tell that the person was one of our custodians. I recognized the huge ring on his left hand. There it was as bold as could be, like the clouds in the sky I saw before. It was the lighthouse with the jewel at the top! He had told me that he won the ring playing cards. I remembered the day he told me. It was just before the school carnival. He helped my Mom and I set up the gym for the event. But it didn't make sense that he was here now!

He reached down to the floor. He moved one of the boxes. After opening it with the key, he lifted up a trapdoor. Then I could see bags full of food behind him on the floor. He lowered the plastic bags into the trap door. Turning around, he followed the food into the trap door.

18 CHAPTER

Mark and Alan were the first ones to come out from under the desk. I stood up and started to tiptoe toward them. Laura and Christina crawled over to the desk. Mark was the first one to whisper. "Hey, we need to wait until the custodian leaves before we can do any more exploring, or we have to get the heck out of here right away. What do you want to do?"

Before we could answer, we heard men's voices right below the trap door. Alan waved his arms at us telling us to hide again. We quietly and quickly went back to our hiding positions. Sure enough the trap door opened up and Mr. Bond, our custodian, climbed up the wooden ladder to the room where we hid. He stood up, closed the trap door and went over to Mr. Grove's desk. He sat on the desk and lit up a cigarette. While he was smoking, I was terrified that I would sneeze. I am so allergic to smoke. I covered my face with my hat and tried not to breathe!

It seemed like a month had gone by but finally Mr. Bond left the room, checking to make sure the door closed. His keys still jingled as he walked and finally we couldn't hear them anymore.

"Man. What was that all about? Who is under the trap door, and why is Mr. Bond bringing groceries?" I asked.

All of us came together in the middle of the room. No one answered me for the longest time. Then Laura said, "What if the person down there is being kidnapped by Mr. Bond? We have to get help. What should we do?"

Alan stopped us from talking when he

interrupted and began telling us to stop getting so hysterical. He sat on one of the boxes and had a pensive look on his face.

Talking softly, he said, "Maybe this had something to do with my great grandfather's note. He was talking to himself saying that he just could not figure it out. Mark was mumbling to himself too. While they were pondering, Christina, Laura and I went through more boxes trying to find something old and interesting. Christina was behind Laura and me. I turned around to show her an old basal reader about "Dick and Jane", when I caught her trying to open the trap door.

"Christina, don't do that. You are going to attract attention to us from the person down ......" I firmly whispered. But before I could finish my thoughts, I saw Christina fall through the slats in the trap door. I heard a big thug and a groan.

I whispered loudly, "Alan, Mark. Christina just fell through the trap door. What are we going to do?"

Mark replied first saying that Christina probably got hurt and that we needed to get down there right away to help her. We grabbed our flashlights and shined them down the trap door. We could see Christina lying on the floor just below.

"Christina, can you hear us? Are you all right?" called Mark.

We waited anxiously for her to answer. Alan continued calling her name. She wasn't moving. Before we realized it, Mark was looking behind the old, smelly boxes and the ancient furniture stored in this room. We all looked at him quizzically.

Feeling the pressure of our gazes Mark looked

straight at us and said, "I need a rope or chain to get down there to help her. Find something, and fast."

The only thing we could find in the room was an old basketball net. Laura started to rip it apart to make it longer.

"Mark, here take this. It's all we have. You will have to use this." Laura kept ripping at the net and Alan began arranging it in a long string-like pattern. He handed it to Mark quickly, and Mark tied the end of it to Mr. Grove's desk, hoping it would hold his weight.

Finally, he turned to Laura and said, "Laura, you have to go down. You are the lightest of all of us. I'm not sure the desk will hold my weight. Alan and I can hang on to the rope too if you go down."

Laura didn't hesitate at all and began examining the situation. She put the flashlight in her pocket and twisted the rope around her hands. I was really worried about Christina and wondered if we should call for help.

Laura was on her way down when we heard Christina say, “Oww, my head hurts.” She was conscious! Now we needed to find out how badly she was hurt.

19 CHAPTER

Laura prepared herself to shimmy down the trapdoor to help Christina when suddenly all eyes were focused on an old, bony hand with long, dirty fingernails that swiftly covered Christina's mouth. Nothing else was visible to us. We gasped and quickly pulled Laura back to the floor of the room where we were exploring. That's when we noticed that Christina was gone. She wasn't at the bottom of the trap door anymore.

Now we were all panicky because we had put Christina in such danger. The worse part of all of this was the silence in that room. None of us knew what to do. Mark motioned for all of us to get closer together so that we could talk without anyone hearing us.

Alan started by saying, "We need to think and fast. What ideas does anyone have?" No one offered anything. After a couple minutes I suggested that we probably should find Mr. Bond who could help us get to Christina.

Mark responded, "No way, then he will know that we are in here." Laura looked at Mark as if he were the worst kid.

Alan was very quiet but after seeing Laura's expression, he piped up and said, "Mark, what is more important? Shouldn't we want to help Christina more than worrying about getting into trouble? It is the right thing to do. I say we send Emily to find Mr. Bond even if she has to call him at home."

"Look", said Mark, "I want to do the right thing too, but we don't know what we are dealing with here. Mr. Bond may not help us. He could be involved in this more than we know."

Finally, I replied, "All right, let's all go down the trap door. Whoever moved Christina can't be stronger than all four of us together!"

Mark said, "Let Laura go down first and then Emily. Then they could find the ladder that Mr. Bond used to get out of the hole." Everyone agreed. So they got the net that they had fixed before to let Laura down. They helped Laura ease herself down. I was so scared for her as she was moving down into a strange creepy place. Her hands slipped on the net and her face was hot. It was quite dark down there so when she got to the bottom, she stood up and took the flash light out of her pocket. She flashed it everywhere hoping not to find the man with the bony hands.

Next, it was my turn. I took the flashlight out after landing on the damp, dirt floor and searched in all corners. Both of us girls decided to walk together to look for the ladder Mr. Bond had used earlier. Laura, pointing the flashlight at the ceiling of this damp, smelly hole, discovered the ladder connected to the ceiling with old, rusty hinges. It was placed right near the trap door but it had to be swung directly under the trapdoor to help someone get in or out of this place.

Laura whispered up to Mark and Alan standing at the top of the opening. "Come on down. We will put the ladder in place for you. Hurry."

They had successfully lowered themselves into the room. Each of them had their flashlight on and had slowly moved toward another door. Mark was the first to approach the door and noticed light shining out of the crack in the bottom of the door. He knelt down and placed his head on the floor. He peeked under the door and after a few seconds he jumped and said, "I don't believe this!"

He told us that he saw Christina lying on a cot and that a very thin old man held a cloth on her head. Christina stared at this person with terror in her eyes.

20 CHAPTER

We were still sitting in the police station while I continued to tell my mom about what happened. She finally interrupted. "We were all so worried about you. Mrs. Lutnam called our house looking for Alan. When I told her that all of you were at Christina's house, she said she had called there and was told that they were at our house. You lied to us, Emily," she complained.

My mom looked straight at me and continued, "Mrs. Lutnam called all of the parents to ask them to meet at her house to decide what to do. Some of us were worried, others were angry, and some were both. Not knowing what you kids were up to, made our next move very complicated. Someone suggested that we search around the neighborhood and others wanted to call the police. Your dad and I offered to begin searching. We chose an area of five blocks so that if the other parents wanted to search they could target another area. If there was any trouble involved, Christina's dad did not want the police involved, yet. So, it was a waiting game."

She continued, "I told your dad to drive near Grove Park School. I looked closely in the windows of the building. I thought maybe, if you were in there, I would see you moving around. I saw nothing but security lights. I told him to drive around back to the playground. Just as he rounded the corner I noticed something shiny in the bushes near the back door of the school. I shouted for your dad to stop. We looked closer and found your bike in the bushes with three other bikes. As we both got out of the truck, we panicked. We looked at each other while we tried to open the back door to the school. Of course, we couldn't get it opened so we decided to call Mrs. Lutnam, knowing that since she was the principal she could get into the school. I was frantic wondering why your bikes were parked outside of school, yet you were nowhere to be found. I was trying to find my cell phone to call Mrs. Lutnam while your dad was speeding through the streets. He looked through his rear view mirror only to discover that a police car was following us with flashing lights. He didn't know what he should say to the cops when he stopped. Finally he pulled his truck over and parked under a tree close to our house. The policeman stopped his car and proceeded to open the car door of the police car. It was then that your dad decided to tell them about the bikes at school hidden behind a bush and that you five kids were missing."

She told me what was going on in Mrs. Lutnam's house as they paced the floor and looked out the windows waiting for us to get back. Christina's mom noticed them walking away from the truck first. My parents walked fast as Mrs. Lutnam opened the door. The policemen were with them when they ran into the foyer and spilled out the story of their search. Everyone's mouth was opened as they were astonished and confused about what they heard.

Christina's dad spoke first, 'Why did you bring the cops with you? Is something wrong? What's going on with our kids?'

She told me that she told them they didn't know and that she was scared. They needed to get in the school and fast. They figured they would deal with the policemen later.

"So what was happening in the school while we were coming to find you, Emily?" my mother asked.

21 CHAPTER

While we were looking under the door in the school basement, we heard Christina. She screamed, "Help me! Help me get out of here!" as she looked into the eyes of the stranger. He took the cloth from her head and ran through another door in the back of the room.

Noticing the old man's escape through another door, Laura said, "Now is our chance to get in there to help Christina."

Everyone began to charge into the room. Even though the door was locked, Mark was able to break the lock by pushing the door with his body full force. I stayed back because I started to think about how all of these events would end. I began to panic. I knew we were in big trouble for taking the keys and for trespassing on school grounds. But the thing that bothered me the most was that I lied. I had never done that before and I felt so terrible.

Alan looked back at me and motioned for me to come. I shook my head and put my hands over my eyes to hide my tears. Alan seemed to know that I needed to talk. So, noticing that the others were busy with Christina, he came back to me and whispered, "What's wrong?"

I blurted out everything to him and as I looked up at Alan, he gently spoke. "Listen, we may have made some bad choices, but we didn't mean for anyone to get hurt. We were only doing this to explore and for an adventure while Laura was here. We are all in this together. We did the right thing by staying here to help Christina. And now, we need to get Christina some help and decide what to do about Mr. Bond and the old man."

I wiped the tears away with the back of my hand and I hugged Alan for caring about me. He took my hand gently and led me to the room where Christina was sitting on the edge of the cot, shaking. She talked with the others in a desperate tone, while I scoped the dark room which obviously was where the old man lived. Suddenly I noticed a beautifully sculpted box that was inscribed with a lighthouse. The lighthouse had a ruby-colored stone at the top.

It was just like the one that I had seen in the sky a couple times before and just like Mr. Bond's ring! I quietly walked over to the box and I put my hand on it when someone's hand grabbed mine. I turned to look up and jumped at the sight of the old man with an empty look in his eyes. I noticed that he was very thin and frail. He had a long shaggy beard and straggly hair.

I muttered to myself, "Oh no."

Apparently the others heard me and turned away from Christina. Looking at me and the strange man, they all gasped. No one uttered a word. Finally, the old man removed the box from the table and placed it under his arm. He put his long spindly finger to his lips signaling for us to keep this a secret. He then vanished into the door he had used before.

We looked at each other and Laura whispered, "What do we do now?"

I swiftly walked over to them and responded in a rather loud tone, "We are going to get Christina to her parents and we are getting out of here right now. What we do about the old man can be discussed later."

Before we could decide anything, we heard the squeal of the ladder being raised into the wall of this pit. We grabbed Christina from the cot and all squeezed under the cot to hide. I pulled the dirty brown blanket down to the floor to conceal our hiding place. We finally saw the boots and heard keys as the person walked into the room after closely looking at the broken lock on the door. We guessed that it was Mr. Bond. He seemed confused and was walking in circles when he finally moved toward the door in which the old man had disappeared. I felt a sneeze coming on because of the mold under the bed, so I buried my head in my arm and before I could do anything, the sneeze shot out. We froze in our places and the man turned toward the cot. He hurried over to the cot and grabbed the edge of it turning the blanket and cot over which made a crashing sound as it ended up on the other side of the room. He grabbed Mark by his hair and shouted, "What are you doing in here with your friends?"

Mark raised his hands up to push Mr. Bond's grip away from his hair. That's when I covered my head and started screaming. Mr. Bond pushed Mark back to the floor and ordered us to stay there and not make another sound. All of us were huddled together hoping he would go away.

Suddenly, the door opened from the other side of the room and the old man came charging out asking, "What did you do to the children?" Mr. Bond stared at him with a look of confusion. Mr. Bond moved closer to us as we were shaking. The old man whispered to him, "I found a young girl who seemed to have been injured at the bottom of the opening to my hiding place. I had to take care of her. While she was on the cot some other kids busted through the door. I have no idea who these kids are or how they got in the school building."

Mr. Bond's voice rose to a higher pitch. "We

cannot let those kids out of here. We have to decide what to do with them."

Alan and Mark seemed to flinch at the sound of Mr. Bond's voice. Alan pointed to himself and Mark shook his head, "Yes." I wondered what they were up to?

We watched as Alan tried to make a run for it out of the room. Mark gestured for us to keep quiet. Just before Alan made it to the door, Mr. Bond threw his hand out to grab him. His hand just caught his shirt and Mr. Bond pulled it so hard that it ripped. Alan kept going but slipped and fell on the floor. Mr. Bond immediately pulled Alan up by his arm and pushed him up against the wall threatening, "You better tell me what you are doing here and who the kids are over there."

He screamed back at Mr. Bond, "Why are you and this old man down here? My grandmother is Mrs. Lutnam and she said no one is supposed to be down here."

Mr. Bond released Alan from his hold and questioned Alan. "You are Mrs. Lutnam's grandson? Then you must be related to the old Mr. Grove who is her father."

"So what? Who is that old man?" Alan inquired.

That's when I noticed his ring again; the ring with the lighthouse on it. But I wondered what the connection was to that beautiful box the old man had tucked under his arm.

22 CHAPTER

My mom interrupted me, "Emily, I can't believe you had to go through this. You and your friends must have been so scared."

She continued, "Once the policemen got involved, I felt so much better. They convinced Mrs. Lutnam to give them her extra set of keys to the school. Your dad wanted to go with them to the school but they insisted that everyone stay at Mrs. Lutnam's house. They promised they would keep us informed. We reluctantly agreed to wait there. We all watched the emergency lights on the police car fade down the street. The moms were pacing the floor talking while the dads waited outside on the front porch."

I waited for her to stop talking and then I finished telling her about our last hour in the school basement.

She opened her purse and took out some tissues to wipe the tears. Looking at her made me feel so awful. I felt like someone was standing on my stomach.

"Mom, everything is okay now. None of us got hurt except for Christina and that was her own fault. Let me tell you what happened," I replied.

We were all standing there in front of Mr. Bond. He seemed so confused. We were worried that he might do something to us because he kept walking back and forth. Finally, the old man came back into the room and told Mr. Bond to sit down. Strangely, Mr. Bond did sit down. His face was ashen and he put his head in his hands while the old man began telling us this story.

"So, Mr. Bond, we finally got caught. We knew this would happen someday," he explained.

Mr. Bond raised his head to look at the old man

standing there with the box under his arm. The old man continued. We kids sat on the cot together staring at both of the men. We didn't make a sound.

Alan spoke, "You are my great-grandfather's brother, aren't you? I remember my family talking about you and a robbery. You were accused of a bank robbery and the policemen let you go because they could not find any evidence. You disappeared. I was only two years old when all of this happened."

All of us gasped at different times during Alan's revelation. Alan turned to us and said, "My great-grandfather's note we found in the old desk is beginning to make sense. I think it's time for one of us to call the police and let them sort this out."

Mr. Bond stood up quickly, turned around and began to run out of the room. Just as he darted out the door we heard a gruff voice ordering Mr. Bond to freeze.

23 CHAPTER

Twenty minutes later we were all at the police station. I was shaking so badly that a police officer brought me a blanket. He didn't know that I was shaking from fright. Alan, Mark, Laura and Christina were sitting next to me against the blue wall in the outer office of the station. Officer Star brought Mr. Bond and the old man into a room next to where we were sitting. They had handcuffs on, but the old man's box wasn't under his arm. As they walked by us the old man looked directly into my eyes. I felt my heart skipping.

"That's when I heard your voice, Mom. I couldn't wait to feel your arms around me."

We were interrupted by Officer Star. He asked my parents and me to meet in the big blue office. He said all of the children involved and families would be there to listen to his briefing of the situation. This was it. I planned to go to jail with my friends.

Dad, Mom and I marched behind the other families filing into the big, blue room. A large wooden table with folding chairs around it was the focus of everyone's attention as we quietly and quickly filled the chairs. Alan and his mom sat across from my family. Mrs. Lutnam was sitting right next to Alan. I couldn't look over that way. I felt so ashamed that I had caused so much trouble for Mrs. Lutnam. I started feeling sick to my stomach and my hands felt sticky as I rubbed my forehead.

Alan's hands were holding up his head as he sat somberly in his chair. No one would ever expect Alan to be at a police station! Mark's mom kept slapping his arms as he tried to cradle his head on the table.

Christina was at the hospital with her parents. Laura sat alone.

Officer Star entered the room with a document in his hand. He looked at each one of us straight in our eyes as the words officially flowed from his mouth. "Well, this has been some night. Some people here tonight will be arrested, so I suggest you call your attorneys", he reported. "I will return in thirty minutes to give you my report."

Immediately, three adults stood up punching cell phone numbers. They shifted into the hallway where they could speak in private. Laura just sat there motionless. She had probably been through this police stuff before.

About thirty minutes later, three policemen entered the room accompanied by three attorneys each carrying a briefcase. Everyone began shaking hands with one another as the attorneys approached the families they were representing. All of a sudden I felt really small, as if I had shrunk to the size of a fly. I wanted to stretch out of my sleep and wake up as if this were all a nightmare. But of course, this was not a nightmare.

"Emily, pay attention. This is our lawyer. You have to tell him everything. He will help us to talk with the Chief of Police," my father interjected. Our lawyer began by telling us the story that Mr. Grove insisted on telling the police. Officer Star told Mr. Grove to wait for his lawyer before he said anything. But he wouldn't wait to speak.

Mr. Jackson, our lawyer told us that Tom Grove had been recorded as he told his story. This is what he told the policemen. "Fifteen years ago my brother, Mr. Ken Grove, was the principal of the Grove Park School.

During that time, I was married and had a son who was very ill. He needed a lot of medicine and we visited the emergency room a lot. My wife always complained that I did not make enough money to support us, even though I had a pretty good job as a bank custodian. After years of being badgered, I finally decided I needed to do something as our bills kept piling up. I planned to steal the money from the bank and over the years I figured I could pay it back. Everything went as planned. I stole the money and couldn't wait to hurry home to tell my wife a lie that I had gotten a huge bonus at work. After driving home quickly, I parked the car in the garage and bounced into the house, calling for my wife. It was very quiet and still. No one answered my calls. While searching the house I noticed a note taped to the wall beside the phone. The note read:

'Dear Tom,

I have decided to leave you. Don't come after us. I told no one where we will be. You will never find us.

Maxine'

Mr. Bond and Mr. Grove were still sitting with their hands cuffed in the outer office. They were visible to all of us as we listened to our lawyers. With eyes pasted to Mr. Grove, I watched him lower his head as we were listening to the confessing of his crime. The recording continued in a somber voice, "I knew I would be a suspect for the bank robbery, but at the time my family seemed more important than getting arrested. I just didn't think about the results of this crime. I went to my brother, Ken Grove for help. Ken encouraged me to turn myself in to the authorities. But I still hoped that I may someday be able to find my wife and son. I did not want to go to jail even though I knew I had committed a crime. Ken finally agreed to help me hide for the time being, even though he knew he too was now committing a crime by helping me. For a while, I would have to live in the basement of the school until we could figure things out. Just before Ken was able to plan my escape, he became very ill. He gave me this beautiful box and soon after, he passed away. I remember thinking, 'What will I do now. I am all alone down here with few supplies and very little food. I will have to escape by myself.' One day, soon after my brother died, I heard a jingling sound. It seemed to get louder and louder. I soon realized that it was keys. I hovered under the old blankets that Ken had given me. But, it wasn't enough to hide me from Mr. Bond. I instantly told him that I was Mr. Ken Grove's brother and to let me explain before kicking me out. He listened intently. I was shocked at his response.

'So, you stole money from the bank and are still a suspect. You have the money stashed down here with you. You need food, water and supplies and you need to be hidden until you can escape,' he quipped with a conniving smile. 'Your brother begged me to take care of you and he promised to pay me, too.'

Well, that is how Mr. Bond got involved ten years ago. He has kept me down here all those years because my brother paid him a good amount of money to keep me a secret and to care for me. He has tried on many occasions, to find the stolen money. Thank goodness he was never able to find where I hid it.

I am so sorry for what I have done. I lost my family. I lost my life. I am ready to face the consequences."

24 CHAPTER

With their mouths opened in disbelief everyone in the room was staring at Mr. Bond and Mr. Grove. Our adventure turned into a nightmare for everyone. The silence became awkward until finally the lawyers stood up to lead their families to a more private area. Laura was still alone and she sat in the big, blue room all by herself. As I was leaving the room, I saw a lady with a badge swinging from her neck rushing down the hallway to the blue room. I stared through the glass wall and noticed that she sat down next to Laura. Laura looked up at her and mouthed, "Hi."

All of us kids had to appear before the Chief of Police with our parents and lawyers. The Chief was strict with our parents and demanded that they keep a closer eye on us. All of us heard the same lecture: to think ahead before we act, avoid peer pressure, talk to our parents about everything, and to know the laws. If older, we could have been arrested like Mr. Bond and Mr. Grove were.

Mrs. Lutnam spoke to each of us individually. I felt so much better after she spoke with my parents and me. I never wanted her to be disappointed in me. But it was my fault for not thinking things through. My parents took away the trip to Disney. I expected that. I apologized to them and told them they would never have to worry about me breaking the law again.

When Mr. Grove stood up to be taken into custody, he motioned for his lawyer to come to him. He whispered something in his ear. Afterwards, he looked at me with a gentle smile. I felt odd as he kept looking at me. I slowly lifted my hand and waved good-bye to him. Even though he was a criminal, I felt sorry for him.

We were finished at the police station. Each of our families, except for Laura's, shook hands with the lawyers and said their good-byes to the policemen. I didn't look up much as we were leaving and I felt flushed. I hurried to get in the truck with my mom and dad. It was silent all the way to our house. I wished someone would have said something. I sure wasn't in the mood to talk.

We went in the house and my parents put their jackets in the closet. I started to run up the stairs to my room when I heard my father say, "This isn't over yet, Emily. We'll talk in the morning." I wanted to ask someone where Laura was, since she was supposed to be staying with me, but I dared not. I dragged myself into my room and plopped on my bed. It was so wonderful to be home with my parents downstairs. I grabbed my stuffed bear and closed my eyes trying to forget about what happened at school. But I couldn't get it out of my head. I kept thinking about what we did wrong, what we did right, and what we should have or should not have done. I wondered what Mr. Grove whispered to the policemen. I wanted Laura to be here with me. Where did she go?

25 CHAPTER

I heard the birds calling to each other and when I opened my eyes I saw the sun peeking over the clouds. I knew it was almost time for my lecture. I dallied in my bedroom keeping as quiet as possible so my parents would think I was still asleep. But it didn't work. I could hear my mom's shoes climbing the stairs and as they sounded louder and louder, I threw the covers over my head.

"Emily, your father and I are waiting for you to come downstairs," my mom barked as she opened the door to my room. I really didn't feel like getting up but I knew I had to face the dragons.

"I'll be down in a minute, Mom," I answered. I grabbed my robe and slipped into my moccasins. I didn't sleep well and I wasn't even hungry for breakfast. I sat at the kitchen table where two cups of coffee were steaming in the special cups my parents use every day. My dad was standing up facing out the kitchen window and my mom was buttering toast as if everything was normal. But nothing was normal that morning.

My father began speaking in a low tone. I hated the sound in his voice. I felt so ashamed that I had hurt him and humiliated him. And my mom, who is always so kind and generous to me, continued to make breakfast for all of us without a sound. That was the worst punishment. She wouldn't talk to me. "Your mom and I believe that you know what you did was wrong. We don't understand why? And we really don't want any excuses. So, in addition to Disney being out of the picture, you will have to make up your other punishments yourself. We will give you until dinner time to come up with a plan to make up for what you have done," my dad demanded.

I answered immediately, "I will. I understand. May I go back to my room now?"

My mother responded, "No. You must eat some breakfast first." Did she have any idea how difficult that was for me? I could barely move as I didn't want them looking at me. I kept my head down and painfully ate my breakfast.

Just as I was getting up from my chair I heard the doorbell ring. I raced to the door thinking it might be Laura. I looked out the window panel in the door but it wasn't Laura. It was a man with a briefcase hanging from his shoulder and a box under his arm.

Opening the door, he asked to see my father. I went to get my dad and when he arrived at the door, the man gave him the box under his arm and opened his case to gather some papers while talking quickly with real grown up words. I saw my dad sign the papers and place the box on the table in the hallway.

As my dad threw the box on the table, he growled, "Emily, this box is for you and your friends from Mr. Grove. His lawyer told me that he wanted you and your friends to have it." I walked over to the table. I touched the box as if it were a treasure. I tried to study it when we were in the school basement because it was so beautiful and because it was the picture that appeared a couple times in the sky. Now it belonged to my friends and me. I traced the lighthouse with the tip of my finger. I bent down to look at the jewel on top of the lighthouse. It certainly was a very special box.

Curious about the contents, I opened the lid slowly. My stomach was in knots. Inside I found two ring boxes. In one box there was a ring identical to the ring Mr. Bond wore. It also matched the inscribed lighthouse on the top of the box. I wondered why two rings. So I opened the other box and it didn't have a ring in it but there was a note that read, 'To Ken, my son, in honor of his graduation from college.' So that was it. One ring was for Ken Grove. But where did the ring come from that Mr. Bond wore?

I carried the box into the kitchen where my parents were finishing their coffee. I sat down and placed the box on the kitchen table. Again, I opened the one box and this time I took the ring out of the box to examine it closely. There were tiny letters inside the ring, but I couldn't make out what they said. My parents were now watching me try to read the inscription on the ring in the box. My mom suggested, “There is a magnifying glass in my desk. Go get it. It will help you.” I jumped up and hurried into the study. Running back to the kitchen my parents were now totally focused on what I was doing. I twisted and turned the ring under the magnifying glass until I could read the lettering. It said, ‘Tom Grove, in honor of his -------.’ The blank was not filled in. That is really strange, I thought.

Noticing my confusion my mom asked me what it said inside the ring. I explained that it was not really finished. After reading the words, my mom said, “Well maybe it means the ring was meant for Tom Grove after he accomplished something. Either he never succeeded or his father never got around to giving it to him.” My mind was really twirling and twisting trying to figure this out. I decided I needed to share this with the rest of the kids, but I knew that was out of the question. Mom and dad would not be letting me spend time with my friends for awhile.

26 CHAPTER

I believe I have figured out the confusion with the lighthouse box and the rings. There must have been two rings in the boxes at first. There was one for each son. Ken Grove must have gotten his when he graduated from college and the one remaining in the box was meant for Tom Grove. Somehow Mr. Bond got Ken Grove's ring. He may have been given the ring as payment for caring for Tom. It certainly was worth a lot of money. My mom told me that the gold in the ring and the ruby on top of the lighthouse, in addition to the diamonds outlining the lighthouse, made the ring worth hundreds of thousands of dollars.

So, Mr. Grove, the old principal of our school, gave

his brother, Tom, the box and the ring that was meant for him. Tom must have cherished it all these years living in hiding. The box itself must be worth lots of money too. And now, the box and the ring belong to the five of us kids. My mom said that I could meet with my friends to show them our gift from Tom Grove as soon as I told my parents what my punishment was going to be.

I thought about my punishment for days. I didn't want to be too hard on myself, but I knew my parents would not accept anything too easy. I lay on my bed thinking about everything that had happened during the last few months and I finally thought of the perfect punishment.

I ran downstairs to the kitchen looking for my mom. I heard voices coming from the living room, so I turned around and started walking toward my parents.

I faced both of them and started off speaking softly, "I know what I did was wrong. I not only lied to you but I broke into school, and was there when Alan took the keys from his grandmother's house. I promise I will never be that stupid again. So for my punishment, I decided that I will volunteer my time at the SPCA and take animals to the visit the old people in the nursing homes for six months.

My parents looked at each other. I couldn't tell if they liked that idea or not. My father commented, "Emily, you love animals. How is it a punishment for you?"

"Remember when I told you I wanted to join the cheerleading squad this summer? Well, I won't be able to because I will have to spend my afternoons at the nursing homes. That is when tryouts and practice is scheduled." I answered.

My mom's head was moving up and down. My dad was very still for a moment. Looking over at my mother, he waited to get a signal from her. She raised her hands as if to tell him, it was okay with her if he was okay with it. My dad turned toward me again and without any emotion on his face, he stated, "Agreed."

I was so relieved that I had thought of something they agreed to. It wasn't going to be torture for me because I really do love animals. I will have to get used to being with those old people though. My next question made me shiver inside. "Dad, when can I meet with my friends to tell them about the box and the ring?"

The moment of silence made me nauseous. I started tapping my foot as I stood waiting. Finally, my mom answered, "You can meet with them on Saturday. For now, you have to meet them here when I am here to listen to your conversation. When we can trust you again, we will allow you to invite them over and no one will have to listen in on your discussions. Is that clearly understood?"

"I get it. I will call them to see if they can come over."

Everyone could come on Saturday. So we got together in the kitchen. As we were all sitting around the table with my mom, I began speaking. I told them the story about the box and the rings and that we had to decide what to do with them. Laura, who had been staying with her mom was the first one to offer an idea. "Let's take them to a pawn shop or a jeweler and get the cash. Then we can decide what to do with the money depending on how much it is."

Mark opened his eyes wide and said, "Wait a

minute. We should get something out of this? We've been through a lot because of Mr. Bond and Mr. Grove. We may not have been caught if it weren't for them."

My mother cleared her throat and stared at Mark with steely eyes. He exchanged a glance and retracted, "I guess we could try to make up for the stupid things we did."

Placing my hand on Laura's arm, I suggested that we donate the money to the Council for Domestic Violence. Everyone's eyes turned toward Laura. Her face beamed with a smile of acceptance. Alan suggested that this was a great idea, but couldn't we get some of the money for each of us for college. Alan glanced at my mom and noticed her raised eyebrows. He restated his idea by saying, "Well, it would be nice if we could have some college money, but since we got the money under the circumstances that we did, I guess we should give it to some charity. So, we were all in agreement that we would give it to the Council for Domestic Violence.

We ended the school year still being the best of friends. We are older and wiser now. Laura moved back home permanently. I love having my best friend here again. My mom and dad actually let me invite the group over while they sat in the kitchen. We kids watched movies together in another room.

It is summer time now. I really love visiting the old people. I have learned how to knit, how to do origami, and how to play piano. The smiles on their faces when I walk in with a puppy or kitten, doesn't really seem like punishment. But I'm not going to tell my parents.

ABOUT THE AUTHOR

Mary Slimmer grew up in a military family who lived abroad for many years. She retired from the Oswego City School District in New York after twenty-five years of serving as teacher and administrator. She has always been an advocate for children and their families and has served on many boards. She has served on the boards of: Friends of Camp Hollis, Success by Six, Oswego Health, Port City Educational Foundation and Hall Newman Center. She is currently involved in teaching adult writing workshops.

16178421R00084

Made in the USA
Charleston, SC
08 December 2012